THE VERY CRANKY BEAR

To Tom and Sam.
    —NB.

Scholastic Canada Ltd.
604 King Street West, Toronto, Ontario M5V 1E1, Canada

Scholastic Inc.
557 Broadway, New York, NY 10012, USA

Scholastic Australia Pty Limited
PO Box 579, Gosford, NSW 2250, Australia

Scholastic New Zealand Limited
Private Bag 94407, Greenmount, Auckland, New Zealand

Scholastic Children's Books
Euston House, 24 Eversholt Street, London NW1 1DB, UK

Library and Archives Canada Cataloguing in Publication

Bland, Nick, 1973-
The very cranky bear / Nick Bland.

ISBN 978-0-545-98616-8 (bound)-ISBN 978-0-545-98614-4 (pbk.)

I. Title.

PZ7.B557Ve 2009   j823'.92   C2008-905180-7

ISBN-10 0-545-98616-8 (bound) ISBN-10 0-545-98614-1 (pbk.)

First published by Scholastic Australia in 2008.
This edition published in Canada by Scholastic Canada Ltd. in 2009.
Copyright © 2008 by Nick Bland.
All rights reserved.

6 5 4 3   Printed in Singapore   46   10 11 12 13 14

NICK BLAND

THE VERY CRANKY BEAR

Scholastic Canada Ltd.

Toronto New York London Auckland Sydney
Mexico City New Delhi Hong Kong Buenos Aires

In the Jingle Jangle Jungle on a cold and rainy day,
four little friends found a perfect place to play.

Moose had marvellous antlers and Lion, a golden mane.
Zebra had fantastic stripes and Sheep . . . well, Sheep was plair

None of them had noticed that someone else was there.

Sleeping in that cave was a very cranky . . .

BEAR!

"ROAAAAR," went the cranky bear,

"ROAR. ROAR. ROAR!"

He gnashed his teeth and stomped his feet
and chased them out the door.

So in the Jingle Jangle Jungle on a cold and rainy day,
four little friends had nowhere warm to play.

"Wait a minute," said Zebra,
as she scratched her furry chin.
"Maybe if we cheered him up,
he'd let us come back in."

"If I did not have stripes," she said,
"I'd be cranky too.
We should give that bear some stripes,
that's what we should do."

"Stripes are silly," Moose complained,
"especially on a bear.
My antlers always cheer me up,
let's give that bear a pair."

"No, no, no, no, no," said Lion,
"antlers are a bore!
A golden mane like mine," he said,
"would cheer him up for sure."

So Zebra fetched a tin of mud
and Lion, some grass of gold.

Moose got two big branches,
and Sheep . . . well, Sheep got cold.

Sheep was getting worried.
"They've been eaten up for sure!"

And then, from in the cave,
there came a very cranky . . .

"ROAAAAR!"

Zebra, Lion and Moose ran out and Bear was right behind them.
They hid behind the bushes where they hoped he wouldn't find them.

"Why is he still cranky? He's got antlers, stripes and mane!
Before we gave him those," Lion said, "he looked so very plain!"

As Bear stormed back inside the cave,
he turned and roared at Sheep.

"ALL I REALLY WANT," he said,

"IS A QUIET PLACE TO SLEEP!"

So Sheep fetched a pair of clippers and she clipped off half her wool.

She stuffed it in a cotton bag until the bag was full.

She tiptoed back inside the cave. "Excuse me, Bear," she said. "Would you like a pillow for underneath your head?"

"Well, thank you very much," said Bear, and soon he fell asleep.
Maybe he was dreaming of a plain but thoughtful sheep.